W9-CDF-631

tweet tweet tweet

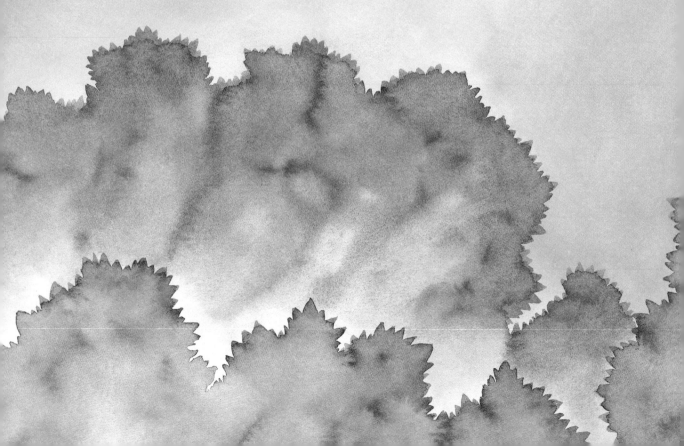

For my big brother, James

VIKING

Penguin Young Readers

An imprint of Penguin Random House LLC

Visit us at penguinrandomhouse.com

First published in the United States of America by Viking,
an imprint of Penguin Random House LLC, 2019

LIBRARY OF CONGRESS CATALOGING-IN-PUBLICATION DATA IS AVAILABLE.

ISBN 9780425290606

Special Markets ISBN 9780593203682 Not for resale

3   5   7   9   10   8   6   4

Manufactured in China   Set in KG No Regrets

Book design by Nancy Brennan

This Imagination Library edition is published by Penguin Young Readers, a division
of Penguin Random House, exclusively for Dolly Parton's Imagination Library,
a not-for-profit program designed to inspire a love of reading and learning, sponsored
in part by The Dollywood Foundation. Penguin's trade editions of this work are
available wherever books are sold.

JUST
like my
Brother

Gianna Marino

VIKING

Now it's your turn to hide.
One, two, three, four, five . . .

six,

seven,

eight,

nine . . .

TEN!

Ready or not,
here I come!

Good morning, Turtle.
Have you seen
my brother?

He's tall.

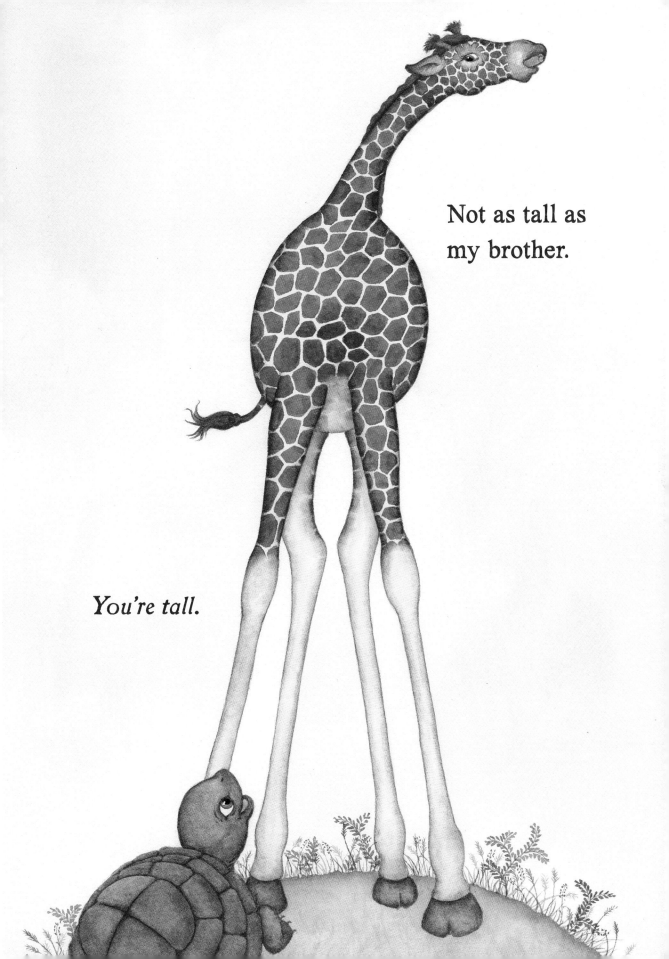

Not as tall as
my brother.

You're tall.

Howdy, zebras.
Have you seen my brother?

He has lots of spots.

You have lots of spots.

My spots are not as big as
my brother's spots.

sniff sniff

whooooooosh

Pardon me, flamingos.
Have you seen my
brother?

He's very brave.

Flick Flick twitch

YOU, *without a doubt,*
are just as brave.

Most definitely!

I am?

As brave as my brother?

Hmmm.
I'll ask the elephants.
They know everything.

rustle rustle rustle

Excuse me, elephants,
do you think I am as
brave as my brother?

crackle crackle CRUNCH!

Watch out BEHIND YOU!

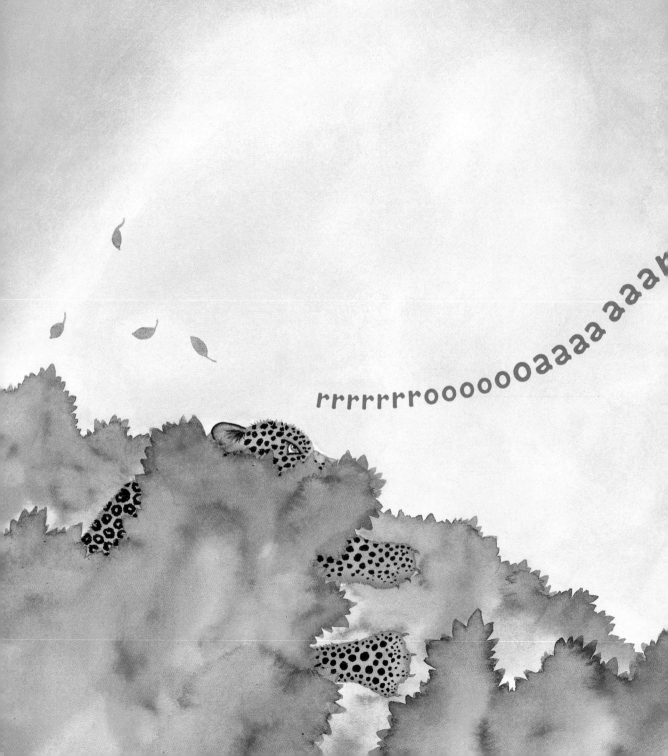

rrrrrrroooooooaaaa aaaa aaar

Oh.
It's YOU, Leopard.
I am in the middle of hide-and-seek.
What do you want?

Um . . .
I was just going to say what a
tall, fast, brave
giraffe you are.

I am?

Just like my brother.

tweet tweet